SPOOKY COVERS

By Michael Welch

AuthorHouse™
1663 Liberty Drive
Bloomington, IN 47403
www.authorhouse.com
Phone: 1 (800) 839-8640

Published by AuthorHouse 10/25/2019

ISBN: 978-1-7283-3262-8 (sc)
ISBN: 978-1-7283-3263-5 (e)

Print information available on the last page.

Any people depicted in stock imagery provided by Getty Images are models,
and such images are being used for illustrative purposes only.
Certain stock imagery © Getty Images.

This book is printed on acid-free paper.

Because of the dynamic nature of the Internet, any web addresses or links contained in this book may have changed
since publication and may no longer be valid. The views expressed in this work are solely those of the author and do
not necessarily reflect the views of the publisher, and the publisher hereby disclaims any responsibility for them.

authorHOUSE®

When the night moon
pops out.

BEWARE THE
SPOOKY COVERS!!!

What are spooky covers you say?

They are covers that lurk at the bottom of your laundry that eat bad people who dont listen and who are mean, but they love eating bad children.

Hee Hee Hee says spooky covers
leave me alone forget about me
cause when you open this basket.

I'LL GRAB YOU AND SAY

SPOOKY

COVERS!

I'll wait and hide hee hee hee
you won't find me or see me.

I can hide under your chair
while you watch TV

Then pop out and GET YOU

SPOOKY COVERS!

When you cook your yum yum food
Mmm smells GOOD ha ha ha.

I'll get you HEE HEE HEE and what do i say....

SPOOKY COVERS!

Blahhhh

Can anyone stop me

THE SPOOKY COVERS

NO!

But wait!..we spooky covers hear there is one who tries to stop us.

The Cleaner!

Run Run Run Spooky Covers the Cleaner washes and makes us smell clean.

YUCK!

The Cleaner finds us where we hide using his spooky DETECTOR.

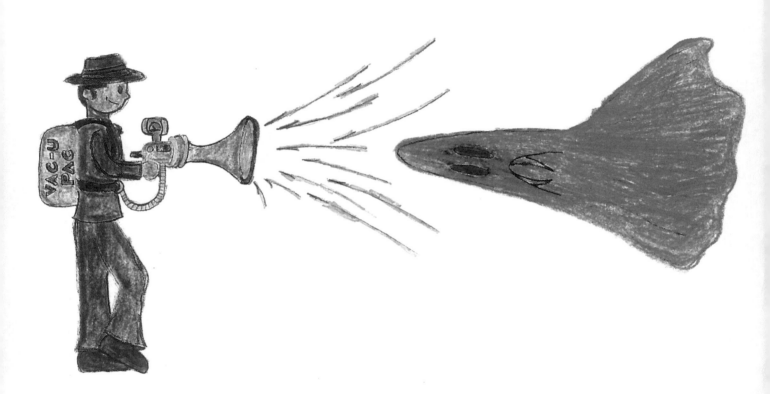

Then sucks us up with his vacu–pak.

Oh Noooo!

No more hee hee but silence and hush.
But don't be sad because when the
night comes, and moon shines bright.

SPOOKY COVERS WILL RETURN
AND BE DYNO-MITE

THE END

Bronx New York is where I grew up in an adventurist place where you could use your imagination every day to see something new and make yourself laugh. Rivers, streams, tunnels, forest paths became my inspiration to touch the sky one day. The elementary school was located near my house, so it was an adventure to escape nah just kidding.

Printed in the United States
By Bookmasters